This book belongs to

Kaylub. Slape

Peter
and the Wolf

RETOLD BY

Samantha Easton

ILLUSTRATED BY

Richard Bernal

ARIEL BOOKS

ANDREWS AND McMEEL
KANSAS CITY

Library of Congress Cataloging-in-Publication Data

Easton, Samantha.
    Peter and the wolf / retold by Samantha Easton ; illustrated by
Richard Bernal.
        p.   cm.
    "Ariel books."
    Based on Petia i volk / Sergey Prokofiev.
    Summary: Retells the orchestral fairy tale in which a boy ignores
his grandfather's warnings and captures a wolf with the help of a
bird, a duck, and a cat.
    ISBN 0-8362-4921-6 : $6.95
    [1. Fairy tales.] I. Bernal, Richard, ill. II. Prokofiev, Sergey,
1891–1953. Petia i volk. III. Title.
PZ8.E135Pe   1992
[E]—dc20   91–34970
                                                                  CIP
                                                                   AC

Design: Susan Hood and Mike Hortens
Art Direction: Armand Eisen, Mike Hortens, and Julie Phillips
Art Production: Lynn Wine
Production: Julie Miller and Lisa Shadid

Peter
and the Wolf

$\mathcal{L}$ong ago in Russia there lived a boy
named Peter. Peter lived with his grandfather in a wooden house with a little garden
beside it. Surrounding the house and garden
was a high stone wall.

On the other side of the wall was a wide
green meadow, and beyond that was a great
forest. Peter longed more than anything to
play in the meadow and explore the forest.

7

Now Peter's grandfather had told him many times that he was never to go beyond the high stone wall and into the meadow.

"Why not, Grandpapa?" Peter had asked.

"Because," replied his grandfather, "if you go into the meadow a fierce wolf might come out of the forest, and what would you do then?"

Peter didn't answer, but to himself he thought, "If a wolf came out of the forest, I would catch him!"

One morning Peter woke up very early. When he looked outside, he saw the sun rising. A little bird was singing in the birch tree outside his window. The bird was Peter's friend and she chirped to him, "What a beautiful day it is!"

It was a beautiful day, indeed!
Peter pulled on his clothes and tiptoed
downstairs. Then he raced into the garden.

The little bird flew down and perched on
his shoulder. "How nice the meadow looks!"
she sang. Peter peered through the gate. The
tall green grass was waving in the breeze.
The pond in the meadow was blue and
sparkling. It was a perfect day to go exploring!

Peter looked over his shoulder at the
house. It was dark and quiet. "Grandpapa
must still be sleeping!" Peter thought.

Then Peter opened the gate and stepped into the green meadow!

In his haste, Peter neglected to shut the gate, and the duck followed after him.

"I shall have a lovely swim in the pond!" she quacked happily. She waddled to the edge of the pond and slid into the water.

The little bird watched her curiously. Then she flew from Peter's shoulder to the pond.

"Who are you?" she chirped at the duck. "What kind of bird are you if you can't fly?"

"Indeed!" replied the duck crossly. "Well, what kind of bird are you if you can't swim?"

Then the little bird and the duck began to argue. The duck swam in circles around the pond, quacking and ruffling her tail feathers. Meanwhile the little bird hopped up and down on the bank, chattering excitedly.

Peter laughed and laughed until he saw something slinking through the tall green grass. It was the cat!

Closer and closer she came, creeping along on her silent, velvety paws.

"Those silly birds are too busy fighting to see me coming," she thought. "If I am quick and quiet I shall catch the little one for my breakfast!"

Just then Peter shouted to his friend the little bird, "Look out! Look out!"

In the nick of time the little bird saw the cat and flew to the top of a tall tree!

The cat circled the bottom of the tree, staring up at the little bird. "Should I climb up there?" the cat wondered. But then she thought, "By the time I get all the way up, the little bird will have flown away!"

Peter was watching all this very closely when a voice behind him shouted, "Peter! What are you doing out there?"

It was Grandfather. Peter hung his head.

"I told you not to go into the meadow!" Grandfather said, shaking his finger at Peter. "What if a fierce wolf came out of the forest? What would you do then?"

Peter's grandfather led him back into the garden and locked the gate.

"I have to go to town to do some errands," Grandfather said. "So stay here like a good boy."

Then Grandfather went away, leaving Peter alone in the garden. Peter sat down in front of the house and sighed.

"Don't be sad, Peter," sang his friend the little bird.

"But it isn't fair!" said Peter. "If a wolf came I'd catch him. I know I could!"

Just as Peter said that, a big gray wolf came slinking out of the forest!

At the sight of the wolf,
the cat meowed and went
racing up the
tall tree.
The little bird
hopped to the
end of a long branch
to get as far away from the
cat as possible.

"Help! Help!" quacked the duck,
who was still swimming in the pond.
She was so afraid that she flapped
out of the water and went
running toward the house.

"Oh, no!" cried Peter, for the wolf had spotted the duck and was chasing her.

The duck ran as fast as she could, but she wasn't fast enough to get away from the fierce gray wolf!

Soon he caught up with her. He opened his jaws wide, then—*gulp*—he swallowed the duck in a single bite!

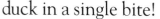

After that the wolf trotted over to the tall tree. He prowled around it, staring hungrily at the cat and the little bird.

"Oh, no!" thought Peter. "I must somehow stop that wolf!"

So Peter ran into the house and returned
with a length of rope. Slinging the rope over
his shoulder, he climbed the high stone wall.
One of the branches of the tall tree reached
over the wall, and Peter scrambled across it
to the tree.

The little bird immediately flew to Peter
and perched on his shoulder. The frightened
cat scampered to him, too, and climbed into
his arms. Now the little bird
was very uneasy about the cat
being so close!

"Please," Peter said,
"won't you both try
to be friends?"

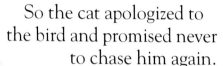

So the cat apologized to the bird and promised never to chase him again. The three of them stared down at the wolf.

"But what shall we do now?" said the little bird.

"I have a plan!" said Peter.

Peter whispered into the little bird's ear, "Quick! Fly down to the wolf and circle his head. But be careful that he doesn't catch you. The cat and I will take care of the rest!"

So the little bird flew down to the wolf. She flew all around his head, flitting this way and that! The wolf snapped furiously at her—snap! snap! But the little bird was too quick for him, and he couldn't catch her.

Meanwhile Peter made the rope into a lasso, which he gave to the cat. She took it in her mouth, and while Peter looped the loose end around the tree branch, she crept down the tree with it—closer and closer to the wolf.

The wolf was too busy trying to catch the little bird to notice Peter and the cat. Soon the cat was close enough to slip the lasso over the wolf's tail. Then Peter pulled on the rope as hard as he could!

How the wolf struggled to free himself! Every time the wolf jumped, Peter pulled the rope and raised the wolf higher into the air!

Just then some hunters came along. They had been following the wolf's trail, and when they saw him, they began firing their guns.

"Please don't shoot!" cried Peter. "My friends and I have already caught the wolf. Now we would like to take him to the zoo. Will you help us?"

"Certainly," said the hunters, who were very surprised that such a small boy as Peter had managed to catch a wolf.

So they cut the wolf down from the tree, tied his feet to a pole, and set off to town. What a procession it was! Peter was at the head with the little bird perched on his shoulder and the cat strutting beside him. Then came the hunters carrying the wolf. Peter's grandfather met them and joined the procession, too.

"Hrrumph," said Grandfather as he went. "So Peter caught a wolf. But what if the wolf had caught him? What then?"

"See how clever we are?" the cat said to Peter.

"Yes," chirped the bird. "See what Peter and I caught! How clever we are!"

"Don't forget that I helped, too!" sniffed the cat.

And if you listened very carefully, you could hear the duck in the wolf's stomach. As the wolf swung back and forth on the pole, she quacked, "Let me out! Let me out!" Finally one of the hunters slapped the wolf

on the back and out she popped, to the joy
of Peter and his friends.

Then the duck ruffled her tail feathers
and quacked loudly, "Hooray for Peter who
caught the wolf!"

"Hooray!" meowed the cat.

"Hooray!" chirped the little bird.

"Hooray!" said the hunters and
even Grandfather, too.

"Hooray!" said Peter.
"I knew I could
catch a wolf!"